D0601877

What Are Roses for?

What Are Roses for?

SANDOL STODDARD

Illustrated by Jacqueline Chwast

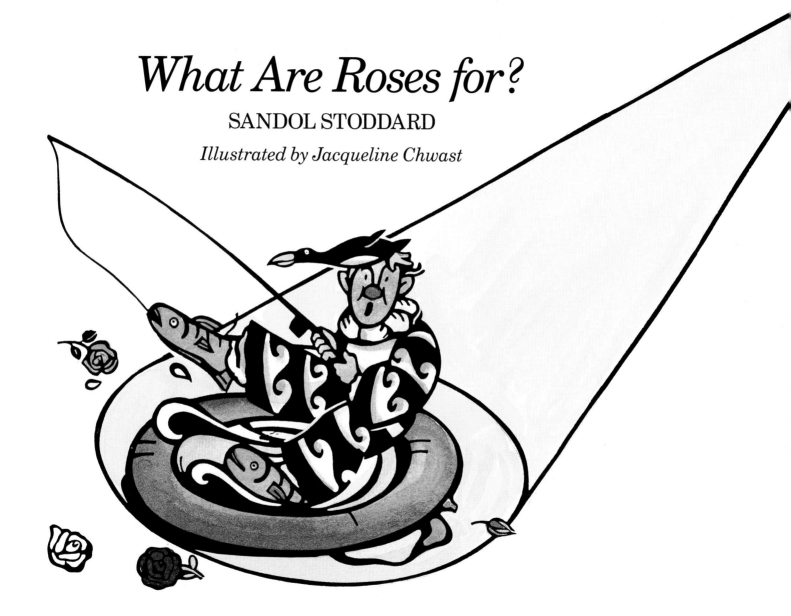

HOUGHTON MIFFLIN COMPANY BOSTON 1996

To Daniel—*S.S.*

For my two grandsons,

Brian Tyler Nemeth and Jacob Lion Macdonald—*J.C.*

Text copyright © 1996 by Sandol Stoddard
Illustrations copyright © 1996 by Jacqueline Chwast

For information about this and other Houghton Mifflin trade and
reference books and multimedia products, visit The Bookstore at
Houghton Mifflin on the World Wide Web at
(http://www.hmco.com.trade/).

Library of Congress Cataloging-in-Publication Data
Stoddard, Sandol.
     What are roses for? / Sandol Stoddard ; illustrated by Jacqueline
Chwast.
      p.   cm.
   ISBN 0-395-74277-3
   1. Children's poetry, American.   I. Chwast, Jacqueline.
II. Title.
PS3569.T6213W48   1996
811'.54—dc20   95-2545
                                         CIP
                                         AC

BVG   10 9 8 7 6 5 4 3 2 1

Walter Lorraine ⟨wl⟩ Books

What Are Roses for?

Noses noses
Roses roses
What are noses for?
Noses are for noticing
    this + that
Noses are for roses
Noses are for sneezes
Noses are for decoration
    in the middle of your face
But, what are faces for?

Faces are like windows—
You reach through them
To find out what's happening
Is that all?
No—

Faces are for knowing
Which is me and which is you
And which is somebody else

Faces are for making funny faces
in the mirror at yourself
Faces are the friendly side of your head
Then, what are heads for?

Heads?
Yes, heads
Well, heads are for heads I win
    and tails you lose
Heads are for somersaults in summer
    and wintersaults in winter

Heads are for a good place
to keep your brains in
Keep your brains in?
Well, brains are handy for figuring out

what comes next
    for example
2 + 2 = four
    give me one more
2 + 3 = five
    give me five

Brains are good for remembering
    useful things like
        where your legs + arms are
But, what are arms for?

Arms are for pushing + tugging
Arms are for reaching + lifting
    + holding + hugging
So, what is hugging for?

Hugging is so you'll know
How much I love you
How much do you?
As much as much can be
As much as the whole world?
Of course
Then, what is the whole world for?

The whole world is for being in—
    being in—
        like a bee in clover

The whole world is for wondering about—
pondering about—wandering about
like a bird in the sky

The whole world is for trying to find out
     what the whole world is for
The whole world
     is for helping + loving + caring
          about everything + everyone
               under the sun
But, what is the sun for?

The sun is for saying goodbye to today
and hello to tomorrow

The sun is for being warm in—
warm as a cat in a lap
as a bean in a pod
as a seed in a flowerbed

The sun is for lying in + dreaming
About growing gardens
Full of carrots + radishes + roses—
Especially roses

And, what are roses for?
That is an important question!

Roses are for roses
Nothing more—
Roses are only for
Roses